SPIDER OF CALICO MOUNTAIN

Jeanette Thomas

authorHOUSE®

AuthorHouse™
1663 Liberty Drive
Bloomington, IN 47403
www.authorhouse.com
Phone: 1 (800) 839-8640

Published by AuthorHouse 05/05/2017

ISBN: 978-1-5246-9138-7 (sc)
ISBN: 978-1-5246-9137-0 (e)

Print information available on the last page.

Any people depicted in stock imagery provided by Thinkstock are models,
and such images are being used for illustrative purposes only.
Certain stock imagery © Thinkstock.

This book is printed on acid-free paper.

CONTENTS

By the Window

ABOUT THE AUTHOR

I grew up in the hills of West Virginia as a coal miner's daughter. My writing started when I accepted a challenge from my mother to write better stories than she had been reading to the grandchildren.

My first story was 'Georgie Tadpole'. Since then I have written several children stories, 'The Librarian's Puppet Plays, a novel 'Take the Wings of Morning' and News letters.

I have one son, daughter in law, two grandsons, step grandson and a great granddaughter.

UNTIL THE TULIPS BLOOM

Dedicated to my sister:
Judy Catherine

CHAPTER ONE

Catherine stood silently in the dark shadows of her father's study. Several minutes after the front door closed and all were gone the sound still echoed in the room. She was going to miss her father for a long time. The house would be so silent without his joyous laughter. Always teasing her until she laughed along with him.

"Now my dear girl you should not be so serious all the time. You need to loosen up and enjoy life just a little."

She was going to hear his voice say these words for an eternity. She was not expecting his sudden death. How was she going to go on without him? This big house was no longer a home and it would soon be filled with loneliness. He wouldn't be here to tell her to put down his work and rest for awhile. "I'm tired and I know you are too." He was gone.

Her sister Cynthia and her family were the last to leave. She had begged Catherine to go with them for the night. Cynthia had been sweet and a lot of help during this time, but she had her family to look after and to get the children in school the next day.

Catherine wanted more than anything to be alone.

She wanted to let her memories flow gently over her soul until comfort came.

She had worked on her father's books ever since she finished college. There would be no more work for her to do. She would be able to give her writing and illustrations all her attention now but was that what she really wanted?

She looked out the window. The moon was so bright and the ocean had a soft glow in the moonlight. I should go down to the beach, take a walk and do some thinking. She still had the abalone shell that her father had brought in from the sandy beach and cleaned it up and gave it to her to sit on her desk to hold her paper clips. When he walked on the beach he was always finding shells to bring in and shared them with her. This was her favorite and would always be in its place on her desk.

Catherine put on a light jacket and walked down the steps her father had built to the beach. The nights could be cool with the ocean wave blowing upon beach. She didn't know how far she had walked until she came to the cliffs. Her father had cautioned her not to go this far up the beach at night. "You can be caught between the ocean and the cliffs and not be able it get back." His words of caution came to her and she turned and walked swiftly back down the beach. Already the tide was coming in and she had to walk in the water. I must hurry she told herself.

She picked up her pace to almost a run. There would be no one to come for her now that her father was gone. The tide was almost up to her ankles when she reached the steps.

She passed her father's study door she would not go

there again tonight. I must make plans what I am to do with his things. Cynthia would be help when the children were in school. She didn't want to do this alone. She would have to go through his files and decide what was necessary to keep. Some she would have to take to the firm and release them to his assistant.

She sat down at her desk turned on her computer and began to type. *How to find comfort after death. Listing the things that will help to comfort you. Acceptance would be the first. Then the anger because the person you love has left you to carry on alone. Then the guilt for feeling this way. Will that be all the feelings I will have to go through? I feel there will be more. But what??*

She stopped leaned back in the chair these feeling were sure to come. All that had set in now was loneliness . . . emptiness and feelings of loss.

The telephone rang. It was Cynthia asking if tomorrow after the children were in school would it be to soon to come and help go through her father's things?

"Of course it won't. We should start soon. I'll see you tomorrow."

CHAPTER TWO

Cynthia came early and had stopped at a moving company and got boxes.

"Let's start in dad's room." She said.

"That would be the best place to start. I have been up there this morning looking around." This was going to be hard for the girls. Their dad had been such a private person and they had seldom been in his room. They had filled one box and was starting on the second when Cynthia laid down a shirt she was folding and sit down on the bed. Come over here and sit down for a few minutes. She patted the bed for Catherine to sit down.

"Catherine what are you going to do now that you don't have dad to work for? Have you thought about going back to your writing and illustrating?"

"It has crossed my mind. But I'm going to need a few weeks before I start to think about my future."

"Is your passport still current? Maybe you should give yourself some time and travel around some. You were going to go to Holland before you started working for dad. You gave up your dream for dad and his work now it's your time. All you would need is a Visa."

"Yes my passport is current for a couple of years. I was thinking on this subject last night."

"Do it you deserve it. I know you haven't worked on your writing with all the work you have done here. Get a Visa and take a year off.

Go to Holland. You wanted to go for inspiration and check out our ancestry. It's not to late."

"There is so much to do here before I can dream about that."

"You can leave the most of it to me. I should have been helping. I should have been here for you. I have neglected the family and I'm sorry."

"You had your own family to take care of don't feel bad."

"I could have been here more. Go ahead and start making your plans. Give yourself at least a year away from all this," she threw her arms in the air taking in the whole room. "This old house is going to get lonesome for you. Start gathering your work and leave this until I'm here with you"

"I will give it some thought tonight. But a year may be to long for me to be gone."

"Give yourself a year but if you want to come back sooner so be it. It shouldn't take much thought and planning."

"Well we will see."

They kept filling boxes in silence and were surprised how much they had accomplished when it was time for Cynthia to go.

"I will see you again tomorrow. Don't do anymore

tonight. I want to help." She gave Catherine a tight hug and walked away.

Catherine took a bubbly hot bath thinking it would help her sleep. But it didn't help sleep would not come. She kept going over the conversation she had with Cynthia. Could she be gone a whole year? This had been her plans when she left college. Was it just a dream or could it happen? She had nothing to hold her here. She kept hearing the words 'now this is your time' Cynthia was right this was her time, her plans and her dream. She could depend on Cynthia to keep her word and take care of things here. She would put most of her things in storage and all Cynthia would have to look after was this big house.

"Alright Cynthia I will go to Holland but not until the tulips bloom," and that was only a month away. She could be ready within a month. She had been awed by pictures of tulip fields and windmills. This is where her ancestry lay. Catherine looked around her room thinking what she would have to take with her for her writing and illustrations. She walked to her dad's room and picked up one of the empty boxes and went back to her room. On her desk sat the abalone shell she picked it up and of course it would have to go, it had its place on her desk. No matter where she was, it had the memories of her dad.

When Cynthia came and they started working Catherine said in a soft voice.

"I applied for a visa yesterday after you left."

"So you are seriously thinking of going to Holland? You won't regret a minute of it. When will you be leaving?"

"Not until the tulips bloom."

"That soon. Good for you that is just a month away. Can you be ready by then?"

"I have already packed a few things. I will put the rest of my things in storage and the house is all you will have to take care of. I will get me an apartment for the year, for a place to work. I have searched for a hotel and found one that will let me send my things ahead, they will store them until I get there."

"Sounds like you are ahead of the game."

CHAPTER THREE

Catherine stood at the gate with her family waiting for her flight to be called. Cynthia's children were at the window awed by the airplanes. This is as close as they had ever been to an airport. They had been excited when they watched them fly through the sky.

"Aunt Catherine is that the one you will be getting on?"

"Yes see the one over there where the people are getting off? When the people are off and it is serviced that is the one I will be leaving on."

"Oh I wish we could come with you." There attention was drawn back to the airplane.

Cynthia put her arm around Catherine's shoulder. "Are you sure you are alright with this? Is someone going to meet you at the airport?

"I'm so excited for you. You don't seem a bit nervous."

"I'm just a little nervous, but this has been my dream for a long time. I'll write as soon as I'm settled in."

The gate was cleared and her flight number called and she was gone. She couldn't see the children as they jumped and waved but she knew in her heart that they were, so she waved out the window.

She was tired from the past weeks getting ready and helping Cynthia with everything to close the house. If they decided to sell all they would have to do is give a real estate agent a key. She closed her eyes and let the past month flow gently through her mind.

Catherine woke to someone tapping her on the shoulder. "You need to buckle your seat belt. We are getting ready to land."

"Thank you." Catherine looked out the window and saw a film of color in the fields below. She couldn't make out the tulips but she knew that was what was making the blaze of color. She would soon be walking among those fields.

Entering the terminal she sat down her carry on and looked around. Someone was to meet her and take her to the hotel. How was she going to know who it was? Then she saw a man holding a sign "Welcome Catherine." She walked over to him and introduced herself. He put down the sign, took her carry on and said. "Follow me."

They were driving through the street and she saw the hotel. It looked quaint and old. She knew she would like staying here.

The next day Catherine decided to go touring on her own. She would like to have a guide but that time would come. She ask at the desk about bicycle rental. She peddled out through the country and to the dikes and fields. She was not surprised at the beauty. It was just as she had imagined. Catherine spent the day going from the dikes, to the fields and the cottages.

She was walking the dike when she heard a voice call out to her.

"Ho miss!"

She turned to see a Dutchman with a broad smile coming toward her.

"Miss tourist?"

"Catherine," she answered.

"Miss Catherine you are a tourist your dress betrays you." He said and smiled at her again and called her name. "Catherine."

"Yes I'm a tourist."

"Do you understand all that you see?" He threw his hands into the air taking in all of Holland and leaned on his walking stick.

"No I'm afraid I don't. I have been here but a short time."

"Felix Zee your tour guide at your service for the day." He said with a half bow. He ran down the dike into the fields picked a red tulip and came back to her. "Each tulip has a meaning of it's own, white for purity, yellow for jealousy, awe then there is red, red is the symbol of love."

He placed the red tulip in her hand. "Holland loves that you are here."

He led her about the dikes, fields and to one of the windmills explaining what each of their jobs were. The dikes were to hold back the ocean from the fields so they could be farmed. The fields of tulips were for the flower shops. The windmills had many purposes but the most important was to pump the water in the lowlands back into the ocean and rivers so the land could also be farmed.

With each explanation she could feel the love he had for his homeland. She began to see and understand the purpose of everything she was looking at and it was all so beautiful as she saw it through the eyes of Felix.

"Are you a real tour guide? Have I got my lessons for free?" She gave him one of her biggest smiles.

"No I'm not a guide. I'm a fisherman. But now as you tour on your own you will have more understanding. You won't have to spend your money on a guide."

"I have done a little research. Should Felix be your real name? You should be called Marijn, marine; of the sea."

"My name was not my choice. Momma liked the name Felix and my papa was agreeable so here I am Felix Zee."

They spent the afternoon together walking and talking about Holland. They walked back to where Catherine left her bicycle and she peddled away.

When Felix was not on his fishing boat he was with Catherine. He took her on tours and call it showing her his Holland.

He took her to Amsterdam, The Hague and Rotterdam and many other places he loved. On one of these excursions he had ask her to marry him and she accepted.

When she moved into his attic room with him she was surprised. He had already fixed her an office space for her writing. When Felix was on his fishing boat she spent her time writing and touring. She had settled in comfortably and was happy.

Cynthia was so excited for her. They sent emails almost every day. Catherine sending pictures of Holland.

Cynthia sending pictures of how fast the children were growing and how good they were doing in school.

Catherine kept her journal every day. She didn't want to miss one memory. Her journal was filled with these memories. She read each word slowly.

Twenty-first. *A heavy storm warning. The skies are dark. The men from the bottoms had met today and assigned who would take turns watching the sea. They had been building a new dike on the northern side of the bog. A heavy gale could be a disaster to the unfinished dike. There will be nothing they can do if the dike is washed away but they can sound the warning bell for those in the lowland. Felix has the one to three am watch. I miss him so much when he is gone at night.*

The lines blurred as tears filled her eyes. The watchman that was with Felix had said the sea seemed as though it grew arms and reached for Felix and drew him in, holding him for a time and then throwing him back. Now Felix was gone. Each day she picked up her journal to write.

Twenty-second . . . *Nothing*
Twenty-third . . . . . *Nothing*
Twenty-fourth . . . . *Today Felix was buried in the soil of his homeland that he loved so much.*

At this point Catherine closed the journal and let her tears fall to the floor. She looked around the room. There were memories of Felix and the things he had built for her. The cubical for her computer, the shelves for her paper and folders. They had shared so much in this attic room.

Catherine put her journal away and went down the steps to help momma Gretchen with breakfast. Papa Zee was back from the cheese market and there would be extra for the meal. Felix always like it when papa went to the cheese market.

"Catherine dear." The soft voice said. It sounded so encouraging. She would like to bury her head in the soft shoulders and cry until there was nothing left. She had to be strong for them. "The meal is prepared. We waited for you." She rose form the chair and went to the kitchen.

They smiled as she took her place at the table. The emptiness of Felix's place could be felt.

"Good morning," they said together

"Good morning momma, papa. You shouldn't have waited for me."

They had learned the 'good morning' since she married Felix and came to live with them. The Dutch greeting abandoned for her benefit.

Momma Gretchen and papa Zee were unusually quiet this morning. Did they sense her unrest? Did they in their wisdom know they could not hold her without Felix? She had become their daughter that nature failed to give. Was her presence helping them cope with the grief? She could never take Felix's place. Felix is gone Catherine thought and shook herself unconsciously.

"Are you quiet alright Catherine dear?"

"Yes momma I'm quiet alright." She couldn't bring herself to tell them she was leaving but they must be told. But did it have to now?

Afternoon she would tell them.

When breakfast was cleared away she sat down in the room with momma Gretchen and took up her pencil and paper. After all she was a writer and came here to Holland for inspiration . . . she must write . . . force herself.

With Felix in her life writing had taken second place. Felix had been an inspiration alright, but he had taken over her life and she didn't have time to write. Everyday he had to show her a new part of Holland if it was just touring the village. How he had loved his homeland and gave his life for it.

Holland was truly beautiful. So filled with flowers and window boxes. She looked across the room at momma Gretchen sitting and working with her needles. Also Holland's people were beautiful. If words could capture the true and simple life of momma alone it would be a masterpiece. She sat there with her plump little form filling the chair. Her hands worked so fast with the needles and yarn.

Catherine watched as row after row was added.

Momma Gretchen would make a good grandmother for the child. Puttering around the house doing things for the child to spoil yet she would demand discipline. The cookies she would provide.

"Catherine something must be wrong?" she said softly.

Catherine was embarrassed for getting caught studying momma Gretchen.

"Nothing is wrong I was just watching you work. I just need a walk." She said folding her notebook and going across the room and placing a light kiss on momma Gretchen's hair. "I just need a walk."

CHAPTER FOUR

Catherine was walking the dike for what she thought would be the last time. She had folded the last of her clothes and put them in a pullman case, placed the necessities in the travel kit and slid them under the bed.

The dike where she first met Felix was calling her to come and remember and store her memories. She was sure she would not need this last trek, her memories were as fresh as the day she had first met Felix. They were burned into her soul forever.

Wind had picked up and splashed the water against the rocks and sprayed her. She jumped back. "You may have taken my Felix but you will never take his child away from me." She yelled aloud. "I will be leaving and I shall raise the child far away from you."

Catherine could still see Felix's smiling face as he waved to her and called her a tourist. Still feel the red tulip in her hand.

She hated to leave momma and papa Zee. She was not sure how she would tell them she was leaving but she must. She had promised herself she would tell them this afternoon. There was nothing left for her here in Holland. Felix was gone. He had been her life. Her journal was filled with these memories and she would read them again and again. She would read them to the child as soon as it was born.

She must get back to the cottage. She closed her eyes and let the chill of the early spring day engulf her tired body. At least the ocean had not taken all of Felix from her. She still had his unborn child. Catherine wrapped her arms around herself for comfort. Was she really trying to give comfort to her unborn child who would never know the tenderness of its father's love.

Catherine left the dike undecided she knew she was headed for a heartache for momma and papa. It was not long until mealtime again and she hadn't helped momma today. This would be a good time to tell them her plans. They always talked about important things sitting at the table. She role played how she would start the conversation as she hurried to the cottage.

When they were seated at the table papa spoke first.

"Catherine we know you are undecided what you are going to do We understand and feel you will be leaving. Would you share your plans with us?"

They were both looking at her. Her role play vanished. She took the tickets from her pocket and put them on the table.

"I've packed and ready to go. It has been hard for me to tell you. It is going to break all our hearts."

Unshed tears came in momma's eyes. "You know Catherine you are a daughter to us. You are welcome to stay. I know also you have many memories and it would be hard to stay. But we have talked and we would like for you to stay. We will not push you to stay that will be your own decision."

Catherine was silent she didn't know how to answer them.

"When are the tickets for you to leave?"

She could hear the hurt in papa's voice. "I was to leave tomorrow on the six o'clock train."

They finished the meal in silence. Catherine couldn't say more.

They loaded Catherine's luggage in the truck. The hurt could be felt. The train was waiting at the depot when they unloaded the truck on the platform

Catherine saw a stork land on the roof of the depot. Could this be an omen for her?

"Catherine will we ever get to see our grandchild?"

"Oh mamma Zee in your wisdom you knew I was carrying Felix's child. Yes you will get to see the child. I will come back for the child to met you and learn of his heritage."

Catherine walked to the platform and was behind the train. They couldn't see her and she couldn't see them. She had not let the men put her luggage on the train. She heard the "All aboard" but still she stood there. Momma and papa was her family now. She had her time as Cynthia had said. Now it was momma and papa's time. The train moved away and she saw momma and papa standing watching the train and rubbing their eyes with the back of their hands. Catherine watched the train out of sight before she walked over to them.

"I'm staying." Was all she could say for a time. "Felix's child should be born in his homeland. Felix would have wanted it."

"Come Catherine dear let's go home."

SPIDER OF CALICO MOUNTAIN

Dedicated to my mother
Mildred Opal
Who's favorite flower were Marigolds.

CHAPTER ONE

Marigold had never felt the warmth of sunshine before on her back in the institution. She lay there squeezing her pillow, refusing to open her eyes and end the warm temperate feeling. The warmth was a secure feeling. She hadn't feel secure for a long time. They told her she had been in the institution for a year.

The morning would be the same routine, bathe, dress, breakfast. The dining room where everyone stared at each other in silence. Every morning it was the same. If she hurried to the dining room she would have a chance to sit with Mildred. She always got a few words of conversation from Mildred.

Mildred had been traumatized as a child and sometimes Marigold felt she didn't cooperate because she didn't want to leave the security of the hospital.

Mildred had never told Marigold that was why she didn't work along with the therapist. She had gathered this information from the many conversations they had each morning.

Then there was Nally, always silent, shaking her head when someone looked at her or spoke to her. She acted like she knew and secret that no one else knew. She would never talk to anyone. Just sit and shake her head. Nally never went to the game room and socialized. Marigold and Mildred liked to go to the game room. The games were simple and childish but they enjoyed them. The games were better than sitting in your room looking out the bared windows or watching television. Some times they would show movies in the game room. The movies were also childish.

Marigold took her hands from the soft pillow and put them over her face. Why did some of the patients look so empty? Did she look this empty when she first came to the hospital? Mildred had told her several times that she looked better . . . wiser. Why couldn't she remember the past if she was better and wiser? She thought to be wise was to remember everything that happened in your life. All she remembered was waking up one morning here in the hospital. Most of the patients wanted to forget or to overcome their past, but all she wanted to do was remember . . . remember. Oh! Why couldn't she remember? She wanted to recall, she wanted to know, to be free from this fear that held her captive. She wanted to go home. But where was home?

The doctor, her mom and dad had told her where she was from but she still didn't remember the neighborhood, the city streets and the friends they told her she had. They had told her she was a straight A student and on the dean's list. Where was all that knowledge now? What good had it been?

"Marigold," the doctor had said, "you are healed, all but . . ."

"All but . . . if only . . ." She said aloud in her perplexed feelings.

She had heard all the "if only" she wanted to hear.

To be healed would be to remember . . . all . . . all! Her screamed reaction was so violent it brought the aids running to her room.

"I don't want to hear I'm healed when I'm not. If I was healed I would remember."

"There is one other therapy we could try," the doctor had told her. "We've tried every resource we have available here at the facility. But it could be dangerous. It could turn topsy-turvy on us. All the work we have accomplished could be lost. All the healing that has taken place could be undone."

"I'll try it." She sounded stern and sure even though she shook inside with the words. They weren't getting anywhere. Therapy had come to a standstill for weeks now. Marigold would try anything new. She wanted out of here . . . out of the hospital . . . to be free for the first time in a year.

"I'll try it," she repeated.

"Don't be so sure. I haven't explained the plan to you yet."

"I'll try it," she screamed. I'll try it," she said with a more calm voice but firm.

"Your parents are your guardians, they will have to agree also. It is not your choice alone."

"Have you talked to them? Have they agreed?"

"Not yet."

"I'm of age. I have remembered and figured that out. Why do I need approval from my parents?"

"Yes, but . . ."

"Unstable, go ahead say it. If I'm healed how can you say I'm unstable?"

"It's not that. They . . ."

She stop him in mid sentence. She didn't want the doctor taking up for her parents. She had sensed their disapproval of something happening in her life that they didn't want her to remember.

"I understand doctor. They want me to remember, but only that I'm their little girl that grew up in a stable home, stable neighborhood, went to a stable school. I was then, something they were proud of, honor student, straight A student with love only for them."

"It's not that bad."

"Yes it is. They want there little girl back. And I want my life back. Why had she said "love only them" was there someone else in her life she loved and they were not pleased with them?"

Would they lose her if she remembered?

She loved her mother and father even though her mother was possessive. She still loved her and always would.

"I understand doctor," she said again. "Will you talk to them about it soon. I don't get anywhere when I talk to them."

"Yes I will speak with them."

She lived this conversation over and over in her mind. The warm sunshine teased her back and forced her to turn over. She yawned, stretched and opened her eyes slowly. She sat up so suddenly it startled her. She wasn't in the hospital. She grabbed her pillow and hugged it tight to her breast, feeling sweet freedom flow through her entire body. Touching the lovely handmade quilt that covered her legs. She let the preceding weeks pass before her. The preparations for her to remember had been made.

The doctor had suggested she go back to the place where the trauma took place. He was ready to give up asking when her parents gave in to his suggestions and said they would release her to the torture. Why had they called such peace a torture? She was at peace sitting her in her own bed.

She was here on her grandfather and grandmother's farm. The birds outside her window were singing and twittering. She went to the window and opened it so she could hear them. It was spring, a new beginning. She had spent many summers here and this was her room. Summers away from the city. Some of the memories started to come back, the pond over in the field beyond the fence, the barn, horses. She let the memories flood through her mind. Would they all come back and stay?

She hoped they came back one at a time not all at once and overwhelm her.

She was away from the hospital, away from the city she had been told she grew up in. She remembered none of it. All she remembered was the hospital, her mom and dad, this her room and now grandma and grandpa and their farm. She felt pleasant memories but couldn't recall them.

Her life had started a year ago in the hospital. Why

didn't they tell her what she was supposed to remember? How was she to pull the memories of her life out of the black holes of her mind. How could coming back to the same place bring back past occurrence once they were buried?

They had told her of her life in the city, British Wood. Still she could not picture it. The photos had no real meaning, not even the stories she was told. But she had accepted them as her life.

Why hadn't they taken her to British Wood to remember? For some unsure reason she felt the hospital would contribute more to her sanity than the house at British Wood. Had she not been happy at British Wood? What was it about the place that caused her to put up resistance, a caution sign.

"I don't think I could take my mother's possessiveness every day." She said aloud and held her pillow away from her as if she talked to it. She waited but the pillow had no answer to her statement.

Her grandma and grandpa would let her roam about the farm and she would be free to analyze her own feelings. Mother would dictate her actions and have her reactions already figured out. Every day would be planned ahead for her without her input.

"We will send you back where your problem began." She remembered the doctor telling her.

What could have happened here at such a peaceful place to cause such a memory lapse, such a breakdown? Marigold had been in the hospital for a year bringing her back to this point. Progress had been slow. She couldn't remember all of the occurrences of that year.

The taunting smell of breakfast continued its journey up the stairs and into Marigold's room, luring her to hurry . . . hurry, reminding her that it was not going to be an ordinary morning of the past year. Mildred would not be there waiting for her. Nally wouldn't be shaking her head. Ordinary meaning the kind of morning she had grown used to in the hospital. No Mildred, no Nally, it would be her grandma and grandpa chatting away with there plans. Today was talked about as being important. She could join in if she wished and could make her own plans.

Marigold went to the open window and let the breeze float in on the sunbeams. A noise drew her attention to the barn. Her grandpa had brought out a horse hooked to a plow. The horse reared and Marigold made a loud, audible sound of fear. Her grandpa soon had the horse settled down and tied to a railing.

He looked up and waved to her as he started toward the house. Marigold looked quickly at the horse before turning to hurry down the stairs to the kitchen.

She went straight to the cabinet and took down the plates, bowls and a cup for each of them. She set them around the table, then went to get the eating utensils from the drawer and placed them beside the plates remembering to put her grandpa's on the left.

The aroma of maple told her there would be waffles. There would also be fresh butter, oatmeal with brown sugar and a cup of hot chocolate, her favorite. Marigold moved about the kitchen with familiarity. She stopped suddenly.

"I knew where things were!"

Her grandma had left the stove and had turned to watch her in amazement.

"Yes you did!"

"Does this mean I remember? Does it?"

"I'm sure it must mean something," her grandpa said. He stood in the kitchen door drying his hands and watching.

"I'm sure it must," she cried. "I remembered where everything was."

Grandpa's voice seemed to bring her grandma out of her bewilderment.

"I feel you will be fine, Marigold, my child. You will be fine," she said.

Nothing, absolutely nothing at the hospital had tasted like this. She wished she could share it with Mildred. Mildred had become such a dear friend, and Mildred thought the hospital food was good. In Mildred's seventeen years she had never had anything special fixed just for her, not even on her birthday.

"Grams! Where is the picture you had hanging there?" Marigold pointed to the bare space on the wall and half rose from her chair. "The picture of the little girl with the ponies, Where is it? Grandpa always said it was me."

"I put it away." Grandma shook her head like Nally, as if she knew a secret.

"But why?"

"Marigold we are not to tell you anything that may

upset you or try to explain anything that would interfere with you remembering."

"Oh please grams let's put it back. It was my favorite picture of all times." Marigold rose to her feet and started toward the china cabinet.

Her grandmother joined her and took the picture from the drawer. She handed it to Marigold. Should she let her do this? The nail was still there, but Marigold stood looking at the picture and fear engulfed her. Why was she so afraid of horses?

Grandma and grandpa could not take their attention away from Marigold. What would this picture do to her? Were the horses frightening her? Should they just stay away and let her alone?

Marigold walked to the wall, found the nail, and hung the picture in its place.

"There that's better. Why did you take it down? I know . . . you are not supposed to tell me why things have changed. I'm supposed to figure them out alone . . . our breakfast is getting cold." she said and returned to the table.

The sighs of relief were almost audible from the two grandparents as they smiled at each other. Their smiles reassured Marigold and she knew she was on the right track. They were not going to tell her anything, but they would not stop her as she discovered facts for herself.

"Do we have to be so careful with each other?" She smiled at them. "You don't have to tell me anything, but can you not fill me in when I discover a truth? Don't be afraid of my parents or afraid I can't cope. Don't be so careful. I'm getting stronger every day. I wanted to come here for this therapy. I wanted to know, to remember."

"We will do all we can to help."

"Then don't think you have to walk around on eggshells. Let's relax with each other."

"And we thought we were to be your strength and help, and here you . . ." Grandpa started to laugh until they joined him. "I'm going to plow the west field today," he said, gave them a hug, and went out the door.

Marigold gathered the dishes and carried them to the sink. As the water started to warm she let it flow through her fingers.

The tepid water seemed to forget its boundaries and Marigold felt as if it mixed with her blood and flowed through her veins to warm her heart. Why had she felt the fear when she looked at the picture of the horses? Had horses played a part in her trauma? The fear she felt was the same fear when her grandpa led the horse from the barn.

"You don't have to help with the chores today. Why don't you just roam around the farm, search out your favorite places and daydream in the sun?"

"I'll help for awhile. What do you have to do today?"

"There isn't much to do. I worked extra hard getting ready for your visit, so we could have all the time together that you liked. Grandpa has already milked and done the outside chores. I have a churn ready. Would you like to churn while I make bread?

"Yes, do you still have the big crock with the wooden paddles?"

"You remember?" Her grandmother shook her head again as if she would like to tell her the secrets that were hidden deep in her mind, wanting to be free.

Marigold took the paddle in her hands and began to churn up and down. She forgot the room around her and the actions of her grandmother. Marigold let her mind drift back over the past year trying to go farther back. The barrier was too great, to thick. Without Marigold realizing it, the dasher became a hammer pounding on the barrier in her mind, trying to get through the obstruction. Each stroke appeared to make it thinner, but still she could not get through.

Harder and harder she pounded until her grandmother appeared.

"You don't have to fight so hard, Marigold. Just gently let the dasher go up and down, slightly turning it back and forth."

"I'm sorry. I was lost in my thoughts."

"It may be finished with the energy you was using in the battle." Grandmother lifted the lid and examined the milk.

"I thought so."

Marigold peeped in also and there was a big yellow lumpy island. They worked the butter down and put it into molds. Marigold took some of the extra and spread it on a piece of bread left from breakfast. The butter was very good and she had made it. She felt an inner glow of achievement. She had helped grams when she was young and came for the summer. The pleasure of tasting came back, the pleasure of helping . . . but would it stay? Would these flashing memories stay? Were these simple, childish pleasures going to bring her back to a fulfilled adult life?

Fresh buttermilk had also been one of her favorite drinks. She poured the buttermilk into the jars that had been set on the table and helped carry them to the basement cooler.

"Now you go explore." Said grams. "You have helped enough for today."

"But I've remembered . . . I've remembered a lot."

"Yes, but now it's time to relax with what you've remembered. Time to play, scoot."

Marigold set out to find her grandpa. He had said he was going to plow the west field. Was she supposed to know where the west field was? Had he said where he was going to plow so she could come to watch him? Maybe he would like something cold to drink she thought. She went to the kitchen and fixed some iced tea in a jar.

Out in the barnyard she listened. He was plowing with the horse and she couldn't hear him. She walked past a shiny new tractor. Why was he plowing with the horse when this tractor belonged to him and had blades for plowing? She crossed the fence and climbed up the hill. At the top she paused to look around. In the field beyond was her grandpa. Back and forth he had plowed until the field was almost finished. He took his handkerchief from his pocket and wiped his face. Remembering his cold tea she walked a little faster. As she approached the field he stopped the horse, welcomed the cold drink, and smiled at her.

"Just like old times."

"Did I always bring you something cold to drink?"

"Always, after helping grams with the morning chores."

"I churned this morning."

"One of your favorite chores. You always had to taste the butter and have a glass of milk."

"I did today!"

Marigold felt like a young child for a moment. She stepped upon the platform built to the plow.

"I remember when you had this put on the plow for me."

"You can remember that?" He looked pleased.

"You refused to plow one sunny day because Gorman was coming out to the farm to weld this platform on. I needed something to hold to while I rode on this. You heated this piece of metal . . ." She sounded excited and put her hands around the handhold. "You heated it while I used the billows to make the fire hot. Then we bent it around the anvil and Gorman welded it to the seat. We worked all day. The next day it rained and rained. We didn't get to plow together the rest of the week."

"Yes you remembered well."

They laughed together at the memory of skipping a day of plowing and then the rain.

"Why are you still plowing with this and the horse when you have a nice new tractor at the barn?"

"I wanted to plow for you today so you could come out and help me and reminisce."

Marigold laid her hand across her grandpa's shoulder and held to the steel bar with the other. Back and forth they went time and time again, speaking only when

Marigold asked a question or remembered something from the past and ask if he remembered?

Most of the time he just said, "Uh, huh." He let her chatter on and on as if she was a child again. Was this why she was remembering and starting the healing process?

She was not fighting her simplest feelings. In the hospital she had tried to fight off her childish feelings not wanting anyone to know about them. She tried to show strength. They all seemed pleased when she was strong.

She was an adult in an adult body, yet she would hurt as a child hurts when Nally's parents brought her 'goodies' such as ice cream, candy or play things. When they had ice cream for a treat at the hospital. Marigold thought it was so good. She wanted some of the same things yet her parents never brought her these juvenile treasures. They would always bring a new bed jacket, pajamas, slippers. Things to make her look good or books to entertain her.

Many nights her heart cried tears of anguish even though her eyes were dry. She remembered promising herself, on those occasions when she couldn't sleep, that she would treat herself to these pleasures when she was out and had control . . . every chance. She didn't care much about looking good. She wanted love, status, achievement and identification. Nally always seemed important when she had these prizes. Everyone noticed her until they were gone.

Only once, at Christmas had her mother brought her a box of candy that she had made for her. Marigold hid it under her bed and shared it only with Mildred. She had wanted to shake her head spitefully at Nally and let her know that she had a secret also. She was fighting these childlike desires because everyone wanted her to be strong. So she kept her secret to herself and put two pieces of candy in her tissue and in her pocket and when her and Mildred were alone she would share it with her. They would laugh at the secret they had. Never telling Mildred she had the treasure hidden.

Some how Marigold knew that if those who held her captive in the hospital knew she was still so babyish with her emotions they wouldn't think she had progressed so far.

They kept talking about her early years and her developmental stages. Trying to imprint them in her individual consciousness. Every time they gave her worksheets, she whizzed through them. All her educational development wasn't lost. She remembered it all.

They said her traumatic experience was still there. All she had to do was recall it and cope. What would her grandpa do if she remembered now and couldn't cope? Would he stop plowing? Would he put her off the plow? What would he do? Was he stable? Could he handle her if she remembered?

"Marigold you've been quiet for some time now. Are you tired?"

"No I've been thinking, letting my mind recollect the past year. Grandpa what would you do if I remembered now. What would you do?"

"Would you rather remember by yourself or have someone with you?"

"I think I would rather have someone with me, because the unknown seems so black, like a night with no stars."

Like the shadow that covered the mountain at sunset she thought.

"Your grams and I will do what has to be done when it happens. We will do our best to take care of you." He tried to sound comforting.

"Why does my emotional development have to be so fitful?"

"Marigold, I don't know. I'm not a doctor, I'm a farmer. I do know that after each fitful experience we are stronger when we make our way through it, and you have come a long way."

"Do you think I will ever be an emotionally mature and well adjusted person again?"

"I'm not sure, Marigold, but I feel that you will . . . and soon."

"Why have we stopped?" She looked around the field. The plowing was finished and she hadn't even known when they had finished because she had been lost in thought.

"Thanks, grandpa." She leaned forward and placed a loving kiss on his sweaty cheek.

"For what?"

"For letting me be a child again, riding here behind you, being myself."

Now Marigold knew this had been her grandfather's plans when he plowed with the horse today instead of the tractor.

CHAPTER TWO

Marigold woke to the birds chirping outside her window. She had dressed and planed to help grandpa today. She went to the window and opened it and let the spring breeze ride the sunbeams into her room.

She saw grandpa at the barn taking out the horse again. She had planned to help him on the farm today. Why was he taking out the horse the plowing was finished?

The horse bucked high in the air and grandpa fell backwards as the horse jerked from his hands. It started to gallop toward the open gate.

Marigold was down the steps, out the back door and to the open gate before the horse got there. She started jumping up and down, waving her arms and screaming as the horse came straight at her.

The horses chest muscles pulsated up and down as it ran toward her.

She didn't run but kept up her jumping and screaming. Just as the horse got to her he whirled around and started back to the barn. The dirt from his back hoofs hit her on the legs. She stooped and put her hands on her knees tired from the jumping and screaming.

Marigold looked up to see if her grandpa was alright. He was closing the barn door. She ran to him.

"Marigold why did you do that? You could have been killed. You should have run."

"Gramps, I could not let the horse come through the gate. It is hard to tell how far he would have gone. You would have had a hard time getting him back. Why were you getting him out today the plowing is finished? Do you really need the horse anymore since you have the tractor?"

"I have sold the horse and plow and the man is coming after him this morning. I thought I would bring him down and tie him to the fence, but I guess he can get him from the barn."

They walked slowly back to the house for breakfast, chatting about the horse and the sale.

They were still at the breakfast table when Marigold saw the truck and trailer coming up the lane.

"The man is here gramps." She got up and went with her grandpa to see the man. She waited on the porch while her grandpa and the man went to the barn. They came out leading the horse and he was coming out of the barn a gentle animal not like the beast she had witnessed only moments ago. They loaded him in the trailer and went back to the barn for the plow. She ran after them and helped carry the plow to the trailer.

As the trailer went back down the lane her grandpa said. "Well that is taken care of."

When they entered the house grandma said. "Marigold

I would like for you to go into town today to the pharmacy for me. Do you think you could do that?"

"Yes that will give me something to do."

"Do you think you can drive the car?"

"I would rather walk it is such a lovely day. It is only a couple of miles to town. It will give me time to do some thinking."

Marigold walked to town and to the pharmacy when she came out there was a man standing on the sidewalk. He spoke to her and ask if she would like to have an ice cream cone. She nodded and he walked into the ice cream parlor and came out with two ice cream cones and gave one to Marigold. They sit down on a bench in front of the ice cream parlor and ate their ice cream and chatted for awhile.

They talked about her grandpa's farm and he told her about his farm and that it was the one next to her grandpas. Just across the little lake that separated them.

"Would you like to ride back to the farm with me? I noticed you walked to town. You can go back with me and I will let you out at the end of your lane."

"That would be nice." She wondered if she should ride with a perfect stranger but he seemed so nice. What would her grandma and grandpa say if she rode with him?

They talked all the way back. They talked about themselves. The ride was so short and she hated when it ended.

"Grandma I met this nice man in town. He bought me ice cream and I rode back to the lane with him. His name is Thorne and he has the farm next to this one. Is there any reason I shouldn't be friends with him?"

Her grandma looked surprised but said, "No there is no reason you can't be friends with him. He is a very nice person."

"He bought me a raspberry swirl ice cream, it is my favorite. His favorite is butter pecan. I didn't get much ice cream in the hospital and I missed it."

"That was good of him." And she smiled at Marigold.

CHAPTER THREE

For several evenings the shadow of the mountain drew her to the fence to watch. Today had been a beautiful day of sunshine and Marigold told herself over and over she was not going to the fence this evening. The shadow just brought fear to her heart and it had not helped her to remember.

The closer to the evening came and time for the shadow she kept hearing it call her name. Over and over it call to her. She leaned comfortable against the railings. She had to wait until the sun started to hide behind the mountain before the shadow would creep down the mountain. She didn't want to miss a moment of the shadow. Maybe today would be the day it would tell her the secret she wanted to remember. She knew the fear would come but she couldn't pull herself away.

Why did the shadow seem so sinister? It was like a giant spider slipping quietly down into the valley bringing harm and danger to those living under its enormous legs.

It would soon cover the valley below and darkness would come. Why did her mind whirl and spin out of control as she watched? Every evening it seemed to speak to her and hold her in its powerful grip. She wanted to run to the safety of her upstairs bedroom but the shadow would not release her. It created a fear that she couldn't slip away from. If she should move it would engulf her as it had swallowed the mountain.

Why did the shadow look to her like it was so evil? She gripped the fence until her hands burned with cramps as it blanketed the mountain and valley below and the darkness fell. There is something about that shadow . . . she kept telling herself. She couldn't help but think the shadow had the answers she was looking for.

How many evenings would she have to watch its sinister creeping before the answer came? Would it ever reveal its dreadful secret that held her prisoner within herself?

Her therapist wanted her here. Wanted her to face life here. . . here is where she had lost her past and withdrew into nothingness.

Here is where she was supposed to try to find it again. But the shadow was so secretive with its answers.

All her mind would let her remember was waking up in the smelly pale green hospital room with her doctor holding her hand and calling her name. She wanted to drift away and never return. Why did they keep tormenting her? Just leave me alone she thought. But now she wanted to remember.

Her parents, doctors and nurses had spent hours briefing her. Bringing her back is what they called it. They had taken her back to her birth, through childhood, school years and teen years using stories. But she remembered none of it so why did they keep trying? They told her they would quote the stories show her pictures until she felt she was this woman again. Her mother pushed harder and harder. She wanted her to look forward to a new life but it was no use.

The shadow held her secret . . . fearful secrets . . . unwanted secrets.

Her grandmother came to the door and called out. "Marigold it's getting dark you should come in."

Marigold didn't want to come in she wanted to follow the shadow and shake it till the secrets were revealed.

She walked slowly through the yard and up the steps. Glancing behind her. She felt the shadow might follow.

"Grams does that shadow that comes down the mountain have anything to do with my trauma?"

"It's not the shadow but yes it plays a part in the problem."

"If it's not the shadow why does it cast fear inside me? How can it be a part of the problem?"

"That my dear is what you are supposed to remember. We are not to tell you more."

"It looks like a giant spider coming down the mountain to destroy me."

CHAPTER FOUR

Just before the noon meal Marigold stood on the back porch and watched the clouds roll in bringing rain. She would be free of the menacing shadow this evening. If there was no sun, there would be no shadow. It would not be calling out her name. She would be able to relax and spend the evening with her grandparents.

She helped her grandmother clean up the kitchen and put away the dishes. They went to the basement and gathered the food for the evening meal. Marigold peeled the potatoes and washed the vegetables while her grandmother prepared the meat and sliced the bread.

"Did gramps go to the barn?"

"Yes he is getting the seeds ready to plant tomorrow."

Marigold looked out the window. The sun had come back out. Her plans for the evening floated away with the clouds. The shadow would come and the menacing shadow would be calling to her again and again until she would give in and go to the fence to watch.

She was hoping for this to be the day the shadow would reveal its secret.

After the evening meal she went to the front porch and sit in the swing and watched the mountain. The sun was coming closer and closer to the horizon. The shadow began to call to her. She walked to the fence and waited.

The mountain was different this evening . . . someone was up there also waiting for the shadow. He was on a horse. That is Thorne! The shadow began to creep toward him. He was going to race the shadow down the mountain and into the valley. She watched in awe as the race began. Where was her fear? Although she waited the fear didn't come.

He stayed just in front of the shadow. Thorne was keeping ahead of the shadow and now was in the valley, darkness enveloped him and the valley.

Marigold draped herself across the fence and let the images take control of her mind. One by one the images came. The shadow had revealed its secret and she had locked in the images.

She would have to see Thorne tomorrow. He would be the first to know she had remembered. She stayed by the fence until her grandparents light came on in their bedroom. She didn't want to talk to them tonight. They would question her and she didn't want to reveal what she had remembered. These memory's would be only for herself and Thorne.

Marigold was up early dressed and went to the kitchen made herself some toast and butter. She was going to find Thorne today. She crossed the fence and walked through the field. She was going to the lake. She hoped that Thorne would be there. She had something great to tell him.

He was there and she walked up to him and set down

close beside him. They both remained silent waiting for the other to speak.

"I have remembered everything," was all she said. Again they remained silent.

"Everything?"

"Yes everything. I could hardly wait to tell you, if you want to hear."

"Of course I want to hear." He laid down his fish pole and turned to her with his full attention.

She told him about watching the shadow come down the mountain every day and the fear. Then she told him about seeing him on the horse racing the shadow down the mountain into the valley and how it almost overtook him.

"That is when my memory came flooding in and the evil fear was gone."

"Is that all you remember?" Again he was silent.

"No there is more . . . much more." You told me you have a son. Is it Andrew?"

"Yes it is Andrew."

"He's not dead!"

"No, but don't be shocked when you see him. The horse trampled his left arm pretty bad. It had to be amputated at the elbow. He is in first grade and doing well in school."

She told him how she remembered him and his farm. How she had helped him plant and harvest.

"Now that you remember what are you going to do?"

She took his face in her hands. He didn't pull away. She couldn't read his face and wondered if she should continue. Then her heart started to pound in her chest and her nerves strengthened.

"I would like to come home if you want me." She said it so low she wondered if he had heard.

"Why would you think I would not want you. You are my wife and the mother of my child. Of course I want you I love you."

"I have been lost in myself for a year does that not bother you?"

"Not at all. Andrew and I have missed you so much." She laid her head over on his shoulder.

"Will you come to grandpa's farm and pick me up?"

"When?'

"Any time you are ready."

"Will this evening be to soon?"

She went back to the farm and when she got to the door she heard voices. It was her mother and grandmother talking. She didn't want to listen but she held still.

"Margaret she is your daughter but I really think you should stay out of this. She is recalling her memories more every day. She knows the shadow of the mountain has more memories. And I think she will get them all back soon."

"I ask you to keep her away from him and you haven't done so. She isn't a farm girl and she needs to be in British Wood where she can have a social life."

"She has been helping Dan on the farm and has enjoyed every minute of it. She even helped with the horse before Dan sold him. Her fear of horses are gone. She is coming along."

"I don't want her on that farm. There is no future for her there."

"She has to decide on her own future. She will chose what she wants when the memories come back. This is why she was sent here She is an adult and you can't stop what she wants to do."

"But I can try."

Marigold slipped back down the steps and ran back up them and rushed into the house.

"Mother what are you doing here?"

"I came to see about you. Mom has told me you are getting your memories back."

Marigold set them both down at the table and started to tell them what she remembered . . . but not all. She went upstairs and started packing her things. She would be ready when Thorne and Andrew came for her.

After dinner that evening she excused herself and went up to her bedroom. She put on her western shirt and jeans. She rubbed her hand down her sleeve and thought how much better it felt than the bed jackets in the hospital and her jeans felt much better than the pajamas she wore in the hospital. She felt like herself again.

She took her suitcases and went to the porch. They all three followed asking questions. Grandpa had a smile on his face that could not be erased.

"Where are you going?" Her mother ask in an angry voice.

"My husband and son are coming to pick me up." She said with emotion. "I have remembered everything. And Thorne knows and I'm going home."

When they saw Thorne's truck coming up the lane her mother gave a sick disgusted grunt and walked back into the house.

Thorne got out of the truck and walked around and helped Andrew down. They walked up to the steps. Marigold was not sure if Andrew would understand. He held out his hand to her and she ran down the steps and took him in her arms and they sobbed together.

"Momma I missed you so much." he sobbed.

"I know . . . I know."

Thorne picked up the suitcases and started to the truck.

The smile was still on grandpa's face when he said, "Take good care of our girl."

"Bring her back to visit." Grandma's smile was as large as grandpas.

As Marigold turned to wave she said over her shoulder. "I will just be across the field. I'm not leaving you."

BY THE WINDOW

CHAPTER ONE

Myself

I don't know where to start my story. I'll have to think for a minute. Will you stay with me while I think? Others haven't! Most don't care how I think or how I feel. I'm not important, I guess.

They talk where I can hear them . . . everyone that comes to visit. As they talk they say I can't learn, that I have metal retardation. . . down' syndrome. I don't feel mental or down. I feel bright and shinny like the sunbeams. That's what Wesley calls them . . . sunbeams.

Don't tell anyone I talk to Wesley just yet . . . no one knows and they may stop him from coming.

I talk to Emma a lot too . . . Emma tries to help me. Emma is such a pretty name . . . Emma means 'nurse'. She tells me that my name . . . Madrigal . . . means 'a sweet pastoral song or a poem set to music.' I would like to ask Emma what Wesley means, but she don't know about him just yet. She almost came to the window the other day while he was here.

The other visitors that come say to mommy, that I won't live to be big. I'm not sure what 'to be big' means just yet, but it must mean to be like mommy. My mommy is different . . .so different than I am. Wesley calls her pretty.

Wesley and Emma both told me at first that I say 'just yet' too much. I hope you won't get tired of hearing it and go away. Emma and Wesley have got so used to it, they don't even mention it anymore. I say 'just yet' because I don't think I have learned and done all that I'm going to do. I don't feel like I'm going to die soon like all of them say. I feel good . . . and since Emma and Wesley come I learn something new each day. Emma is going to bring some books sometime and read to me. Oh! I hope no one knows . . . you won't tell . . . will you?

Sometimes at night when mommy puts me to bed, I can't sleep. I lay and think or Emma tells me it is thinking.

She tells me that I picture things in my mind that has happened or something I want to happen. Most of my thinking is fearful.

I'm afraid Emma will catch Wesley coming and tell . . . or Wesley may tell about Emma. Mommy might catch one of them and watch me more closely. What if she caught both of them? What would she do? Would she make me stay in my room all the time? I like it here in my chair by the window. Mommy calls the room where I sleep my room.

I have only been in three rooms of our house, my bedroom that's where I sleep and think. I think a lot in my chair here by the window while I watch every thing.

Let me tell you some of the things I like. The rain it's nice. It keeps mommy in the house with me. When it hits my window it makes little streaks from top to bottom. Sometimes I follow it with my fingers but most of the time it runs ahead of me and drips off. One day the window was open and I put my hand out and let the rain fall on it. The rain was cold not like my bathwater at all, its warm. The only thing I don't like about the rain is, Emma and Wesley don't come. It gets lonely when they don't come . . . or Emma said it was 'lonely' that I feel.

I like the warm sunshine too. Mommy leaves the window open and I can hear the music of the birds. Wesley tries to sing like the birds. He calls it mocking them . . . he's not as good as they are.

One day someone came to visit. They had a little girl with them . . . littler than I am. I heard mommy ask them how old she was. She was two years old. Mommy said what a pretty baby she was. No one has ever said that to me. I must not be pretty.

I've thought about this for a long time but Emma said someday I will see for myself. Emma said I had changed since I've learned to talk.

The little girl . . . baby . . . two years old, had a doll with her. She left it lay in the floor when they went into another room. Mommy don't know I can walk yet so I slipped over and got the doll and hid it under the pillow in my chair. They made such a fuss over it when they were ready to go and couldn't find it.

There was something inside of me that told me to keep it. I just couldn't let them have it. I wanted that doll more than anything. I had never had anything like it . . . so soft . . . so cuddly.

I take the doll out only when I know I'm alone and won't be caught. I hold it tight against my front. Like mommy does me sometimes. Then I sit it in the window to watch with me.

Wesley calls holding the doll a hug. Sometimes he holds his toys close to him and I ask him what he is doing? He says hugging them.

At night when I can't sleep I think of the doll, there under my pillow. I would like to have it here in bed with me. We could talk together. But I'm afraid I would go to sleep and not get it back in the chair under the pillow before mommy wakes up. She wakes up early.

Well you've let me chatter on and on and haven't gone. The question is still here . . . where will I start my story . . . the only place I know is, where it all started . . . here . . . here by the window.

CHAPTER TWO

Mommy

I have become aware of a lot of things and for me they all started, here by the window.

I would like to tell you about my mommy first.

Every morning mommy gets up early. Sometimes I wake up first but I don't get up. I lay and listen to the noise mommy makes. Then she comes in and wakes me. I pretend I'm asleep sometimes just to hear her gentle voice call my name. She will say, "Madrigal . . . Madrigal, my little one, time to wake up."

My name sounds so soft with her voice. Sometimes she touches my shoulder or pets my hair as she whispers my name. I wish I could tell her how much I like to hear her voice and have her near me.

She helps me up and takes me to the bathroom and washes my face and hands. She's so gentle . . . always . . . even when I don't hold still.

When mommy gets me dressed, she gives me a hug and puts me in my chair by the window. Sometimes mommy holds me so tight and so long I'm afraid I can't

Jeanette Thomas

get another breath. It's like she don't want to let go of me. I'm all she has, you know.

She goes away and I hear clanging noise and smell good smells. I know it won't be long before I get something to eat. I always feel better when I eat. Even thought the food smells good it doesn't always taste good in my mouth. Sometimes I spit it back out. Mommy talks sweetly to me and after several tries, she gets me to eat it. I don't mean to be stubborn . . . I like to please mommy. Sometimes when she looks at me her eyes smile at me . . . especially after one of my stubborn times.

When I don't feel good and don't cooperate, it makes me feel worse because it gives mommy a hard time. Other times she looks at me like I have wounded her but she gives me a hug and goes back to her work.

I listen close to the visitors when they come. They tell mommy, daddy only left because he couldn't face the thoughts of me being retarded . . . he couldn't get his mind to accept it. He wanted a son. That also disappointed him. It was more than he could take. Mommy sits and cried for a long time after they go. I feel sad because I think I have hurt her and made her sad.

I watch mommy through the window, sometime she hangs up our clothes, sometimes she mows the grass. I like to see my clothes hang on the line

The wind that sweeps across my face and cools it makes my clothes dance. I wish I could dance like my clothes dance. If mommy would hang me on the line would the wind blow me? Would I dance?

I wish I could go outside and help mommy. But I feel

that I'm helping her more by sitting here where she can see me. Sometimes she waves at me when she sees me watching her. I smile and she seems relieved.

I know mommy gets tired of just me, day after day. I wish I could tell her about Wesley and Emma so she could enjoy them like I do.

When the weather is bad outside, mommy stays in with me. She will get a cover and put over me and she will get a cover and curl up on the couch with a book. Sometimes I nap but other times I just pretend to nap and watch mommy through little cracks I make with my eyes shut. When mommy gets tired of reading she will hold the book down some and watch me. Sometimes tears run down her face as she watches me.

I would like to take the doll from hiding and play with it when mommy's here but I don't dare. Something tells me that mommy would take the doll and I would never get to see it again. I think mommy would be disappointed with me. And maybe her eyes wouldn't smile at me if she knew.

When I first saw Wesley . . . he's smaller than I am you know and he can walk . . . that's what he calls it . . . walk. I wanted to walk more.

Maybe that's what it means 'to be big'. If I could walk maybe I could go out and jump around like Wesley does.

When I was alone one day, I tried but fell in the floor. Mommy came in the room and found me in the floor because I couldn't get up. She picked me up and hugged and hugged me. I was afraid she would tie me in my chair like she used to do when I was smaller, but she didn't. Every day now I practice walking. I use my chair to hold on to so I won't fall. I walk around and around my chair.

I would like to tell my mommy about standing on my legs . . . they are so wobbly. One day she looked at the bottom of my shoes and then just stood there and looked at me for a long time. That night when she took my shoes off my feet I saw scuff marks on the bottom. Do you think she knows about me walking?

I wish I could bring more smiles to mommy's face . . . like I do to Emma and Wesley's. When mommy smiles at me or someone else the visitors that come . . . it is a sad sort of smile . . . not like Emma or Wesley's at all.

One day when mommy was giving me a bath, I took the cap from the shampoo bottle and filled it with water and poured it over my head. I wanted to make it like the rain that Wesley tried to catch in his mouth. I put out my tongue and tried to catch the water as it run down my face.

"Madrigal, you must not try to drink your bathwater," she said.

She held my face between her hands and that was the nicest smile my mommy ever gave to me before she found out about my secret life . . . here . . . by the window.

CHAPTER THREE

Wesley

I didn't like Wesley the first time he came to my window, but now I do. The first time he came he laughed at me. It hurt. I don't know why but it did.

Wesley jumped around in the yard talking to me and when I didn't answer him he started yelling. I was afraid mommy was going to hear him, but I couldn't tell him. I couldn't talk just yet. Wesley has helped me a lot but not at first.

He jumped around yelling, "cat got your tongue . . . cat got your tongue." It made me angry and I wanted to hit him, or that's what Emma tells me it was . . . angry. I didn't want Wesley yelling at me. I had never been yelled at before but I knew I didn't want him doing it. I made faces at him but it just made him yell and laugh more. He finally stopped and stared at me for a long time. I felt a tear slipping its way into my eyes.

"Can't you talk?" Wesley ask shyly.

I shook my head so wildly even with Wesley's coaxing I couldn't stop. He started talking so sweet and almost climbed up the wall and into the window. All I wanted was my mommy to hold me but I could hear the lawn mower in the back.

Wesley slipped down out of sight and disappeared. I was so glad he was gone.

I took my doll from under the pillow and held it tight against me. Soon with my thinking and not feeling alone anymore, my body quit shaking and I felt serene.

The next day Wesley came again. I started to shake my head but he said

"No, no I won't hurt you."

I knew what 'to hurt' was. I wanted to smile at him but was afraid. Afraid he would start yelling again.

"Hi, my name is Wesley. I'm five years old. I like to play."

I tilted my head and looked at him. I didn't know what five years old was just yet, or to play.

He seemed to understand, and had accepted the idea that I couldn't talk. He had brought some toys with him and he climbed up into the window. He let me play with a toy he called a truck. It had little wheels that rolled when I pushed it on the arm of my chair.

I wanted to hide it and keep it too, but Wesley promised to bring it with him again the next day.

Wesley came once when it was raining. Mommy was on the couch reading . . . this time she was really reading, not watching me. Wesley had been across the street at one of his friends. He comes and goes across out yard now. I know mommy or Emma is going to catch him sometime.

He stopped and made faces at me. I delight in the way he frolicks around now. I know he isn't making fun of me any more He just wants to entertain me . . . and he does. Time goes so much faster when he comes to play. I know what play is now.

I didn't pay much attention to him or make faces back at him like I usually do, so he knew mommy was in the room. So he jumped around for awhile. When he stood still and let the rain run down his face. He stuck out his tongue and tried catch the drops. When he was wet all over he shook like a dog . . . or that is the way Wesley has told me a dog shakes. Drops of water flew in all directions. I almost laughed at him, but mommy would have heard . . . come to see . . . and Wesley would have been found out. It was hard for me not to laugh. Wesley and I laugh together a lot of times anymore.

Wesley asks a lot of questions. Questions I don't have answers for. Wesley is the reason I've learned to talk some. He held up one of his toys and kept saying "car. . . car . . . car." Until I tried saying it. The first sound that came from my mouth, my hand flew to my mouth and I tried to hold the sound in. It was horrible. Wesley kept saying it over and over until I was saying "car" all right. Each time he comes he teaches me a new word. I guess they were already in my head. Wesley just makes me bring them out.

I don't have to practice so hard on a new word anymore.

Wesley tells me what it's like to be five years old. He don't get to be by himself much. There's always someone watching him. His mommy lets him go across the road to play with his friend. When he is supposed to be over there he leaves early and comes to talk to me.

He has some toys he calls "plushies." I like for him to bring them when he comes to play. They are soft. One is a rabbit, it's my favorite. Wesley knows I like it best and he brings it often.

Wesley is sitting in the window now holding the rabbit and I see Emma coming. I want to tell him but it's to late, she has already seen him.

He jumps when she said to him, "Wesley what are you doing?"

My heart cried out! Oh pretty Emma don't make him go away. Without him, my day would be so very long . . . here by the window.

CHAPTER FOUR

Emma

Emma . . . you will have to be patient with me while I search in my head for words to tell you about Emma. I will have to find choice words to describe her . . . more fancy words. She is more grown up than Wesley. She don't jump around in the yard and frolic like he does. She is bigger but not as big as mommy. Emma tells me she is fifteen years old.

As I told you before her name means 'nurse' one who cares for the sick . . . to take care of. She told me that.

I watched Emma pass by my window day after day, before she stopped to talk to me.

The first day she stopped she had candy in her pocket. She gave it to me. It was good. I had never had candy like it before. It left a cool taste in my mouth for a long time.

Emma didn't laugh or jump around the first time she saw me, like Wesley did. She seemed to know what was wrong with me. Emma helped me to know that I'm different . . . special . . . is what she said. I'm nothing to be afraid of . . . to run away from, like daddy did. Emma said there were lots of children like me. But we don't live long.

I watched Emma go by, she had on a red and white apron every day. She has told me now that she is a 'candy – stripper' and takes care of people. That's what they call her at the hospital where she works. She does volunteer work She likes helping people. When she gets to telling me about things that happen at the hospital, I get excited. I can almost see the lights in the halls . . . what ever a hall is as they go on and off . . . everyone running back and forth to see what the people want. Patients . . . is what Emma calls them.

The ones like me need a lot of attention. I don't need a lot of people running after me just because I can't take care of myself.

The first time Emma came to my window, I didn't talk much even though Wesley had already taught me lots of words. She didn't stay long. Now I know it must have been because I wouldn't talk to her. I was still afraid . . . of strangers . . . that's what Emma calls people that we don't know.

Every day now Emma stops by with a story to tell about her work often she brings me something. I watch the shadows on the lawn so I will know when it is time for her to come down the street.

I would like to tell you some of Emma's characteristics, even though I'm just learning what they mean. She is versatile and has a lot of imagination. She can be my friend and still make Wesley feel welcome. She knows about Wesley now. Sometimes they come at the same time. Wesley likes to listen to Emma's stories she tell us. He listens and don't jump around so much. Sometimes his jumping around annoys me . . . just sometimes . . . when I have a day that I don't feel good. Emma always seems to know when I don't feel good . . . and she tells stories to keep Wesley quiet. Sometimes she sings songs and sometimes she sings her stories. She has a great inventiveness, most of the stories she makes up herself to suit the situation.

She must be really intelligent to do that. I couldn't do something like that. Sometimes when Emma is not here Wesley tries to tell her stories and he tries to act them out as Emma would . . . but he forgets easy and has to stop in the middle when he can't remember. I'm getting better at remembering and sometimes I can say a word or sentence that helps Wesley remember Emma's story.

Wesley can't read yet but he brings books and we look at the pictures and he makes up a story to go with the pictures. I know he makes it up because when Emma reads it . . . it's not the same as Wesley's story.

Emma has a nickname for Wesley. She calls him 'squirmmal'. He calls her 'nursie'. They like each other.

I think 'nursie' suits her real well because she enjoys taking care of others. I have learned to say nursie and call her that sometimes.

She is tender and it seems the sun is brighter when she is around with us . . . even when she scolds . . . she scolds Wesley when he makes me nervous.

When Emma works on the children's ward . . . that's where the sick children are . . . she comes home sad. When she tells me about some of the boys and girls she cries. On those days she don't stay very long to talk to me. I would like to help her forget her day but the more she looks at me on those days the sadder she gets. Even Wesley gets on her nerves. But, I wait here by the window and watch the shadows every day. Even if she is sad and don't want to talk, I still want Emma to come.

CHAPTER FIVE

Together

I see Emma talking to mommy, out by the clothes line. They are looking at me . . . both of them . . . I feel afraid . . . I try to hide. Will Emma tell mommy about Wesley? I'm glad for some reason that mommy knows about Emma. If Emma tells about herself and Wesley coming to the window to see me, will mommy make them stop coming? I think that is why I'm so afraid. It would be so lonesome if they could not come again. What would I do without them coming to visit me?

My doll is a pleasure but I like talking . . . laughing . . . and learning.

Mommy and Emma are coming this way. They are smiling . . . and her comes Wesley! Mommy is putting her arm around him. Oh! I'm so overjoyed but frightened.

Mommy talked to Emma, Wesley and me. She started to turn and go when I saw her look at my doll . . . Linda . . . Emma had named her for me. It meant 'pretty one'.

"Madrigal! What is this.?"

I had never heard such hurt in my mommy's voice. I wanted her to know I needed the doll . . . to hold . . . just like she would hold me . . . sometimes . . . tight . . . like she would never let me go. I don't remember grabbing the doll and wrapping my arms tight around her . . . but I remember screaming. My doll . . . my baby, my Linda . . . my pretty one.

"Madrigal? You're talking."

Wesley came and put his arms around me.

"And . . . I taught her." His voice echoed in my ears. He had taught me and he was proud.

Oh, what would mommy do?

"Madrigal." Mommy sounded calm. "This isn't Linda. Remember this is Savanna . . . remember the day Joy lost her?"

I remembered, but Joy hadn't lost her, I had hid her. Only because I was so excited about mommy finding out about Emma and Wesley, I had been neglectful and forgotten about her sitting in the window. Would mommy take her away and give her back to Joy?

"Madrigal, you may keep Savanna until I can get you a doll just like her, then you must give her back to Joy. You can call your doll Linda and she will be your Linda . . . not Savanna."

Somehow what mommy was saying sounded good, but still I held the doll tight. I wouldn't let go until I had a Linda. I wouldn't have to hide my doll anymore. I worried about her under my pillow. Could she breathe . . . did it hurt for me to sit on her? Tonight I could sleep with her. We would talk until I went to sleep.

I didn't have to be afraid anymore. I was free. Wesley

and Emma still came every day. They would wave at mommy when they saw her.

Emma has talked mommy into letting her stay with me while she goes shopping. Emma calls it baby-sitting. It must be my new doll, Linda she is baby-sitting with . . . I'm no baby. Sometimes Wesley comes too.

The first time I watched mommy go away I almost cried. I felt like she was going to leave me . . . just like daddy did. Emma seemed to understand and she kept me busy listening to her until mommy was out of sight. Then she would read me books. I would glance out the window when Emma wasn't looking. It seemed like such a long time mommy was gone. She brought me back a stuffed bunny . . . I don't have to give it up. Now I have two toys . . . but my read-headed Linda is still my special delight.

Mommy, Emma, Wesley and myself have had a lot of fun this summer. We have gone to a lot of places . . . the zoo . . . the park, the river . . . and to the city. I liked the picnic best of all.

Linda, bunny and I sat on a quilt while mommy, Emma and Wesley played ball. It was good to see mommy laugh and play. Emma has been very good for mommy . . . as good as she has been for me.

The fall seemed like a quiet time . . . all the colored leaves falling from the trees. Every one seems so sad. Wesley has started to a day-school and Emma has gone back to school. They don't come as often now but I have my toys.

Emma is busy most evenings at the hospital. But on

weekends, Emma rents a chair with big wheels, from the hospital and we have fun. I ride in the chair. Emma will throw the colorful leaves at me. I laugh and bat them away.

Winter is here and we just had a Christmas party. Wesley and Emma came. Mommy dressed me in my pretty new red dress. Emma took lots of pictures.

Our Christmas party was fun but it has tired me.

I didn't feel like I was going to die soon when my story first started. I thought I wanted to learn, but now I know I just wanted to love. Wesley and Emma have helped me do both of these . . . love and learn. They are what Emma calls 'bosom-friends' those you hold the closest to your heart. I will never forget them.

Wesley and Emma have gone. They will miss me for awhile.

Wesley has his little friend across the street and he will soon forget. Just as his name means 'from the west meadow' he will soon be back in the play fields. He was sent my way to begin the healing process . . . to draw me out of myself with his young energy. The time will come when he won't even remember . . . but I will remember.

Emma . . . Emma is sentimental and will remember me for a long time. She will see me and my features in all the down-syndrome children she works with for a long, long time. She tells me that is what she is going to do now . . . work with children . . . handicapped children. Oh, she will be good.

She has a tenacious memory, lots of love for home and family. I think it is because of me that she has decided to work with handicapped children. And it makes me feel like I have helped the children she will work with too, although I will never get to be with them.

When Emma has a duty to perform she is responsible and never cares what others think when she gets close to those she tries to help. She has turned my rocking chair into a paradise.

Emma will weep often for me . . . Wesley will not understand.

She has helped mommy so much. Emma will remember me and tell of me . . . and I will remember.

I don't care so much about leaving mommy now that she has Emma and Wesley to look after her.

Mommy . . . mommy will miss me . . . and never forget . . . she will love forever my memory.

You have listened to my story and haven't wanted to leave. You will remember.

I hear mommy in the kitchen putting things away before she puts me in my bed. She won't have to put me in my bed again after tonight.

My time is near and I want it to end just as it started . . . here . . . by . . . the . . . window.

Printed in the United States
By Bookmasters